Appleville Elementary

Fire Alarm!

Be sure to read all of the books about
Appleville Elementary School!

Appleville Elementary

Fire Alarm!

by **Nancy Krulik**
illustrated by **Bernice Lum**

SCHOLASTIC INC.
New York   Toronto   London   Auckland   Sydney
Mexico City   New Delhi   Hong Kong   Buenos Aires

For AnnMarie,
editor extraordinaire!

No part of this publication may be reproduced, stored in a retrieval system, or transmitted in any form or by any means, electronic, mechanical, photocopying, recording, or otherwise, without written permission of the publisher. For information regarding permission, write to Scholastic Inc., Attention: Permissions Department, 557 Broadway, New York, NY 10012.

ISBN-13: 978-0-545-11774-6
ISBN-10: 0-545-11774-7

Copyright © 2009 by Nancy Krulik
Published by Scholastic Inc.
SCHOLASTIC, LITTLE APPLE, and associated logos are trademarks and/or registered trademarks of Scholastic Inc.

12 11 10 9 8 7 6 5 4 3   9 10 11 12 13 14/0

Printed in the U.S.A.
First printing, August 2009
Book design by Yaffa Jaskoll

Chapter 1
Hide-and-Seek

"Five, four, three, two, one!" Albert shouted. "Ready or not, here I come!"

Albert opened his eyes. He began to look for his friends on the playground. But the other first graders were not easy to find. They were very good hiders.

Luckily, Albert was a good seeker. He saw a silver ballerina crown. It was sticking up from behind the bench. Now Albert knew where Marika was hiding.

"I found you!" Albert called out. He tagged Marika.

"How did you know where I was?" Marika asked.

"I'm just good at this game," Albert said.

Marika had been tagged. That meant she wasn't a hider anymore. She was a seeker like Albert.

2

Marika knew who to find first. She knew where Carlos was hiding.

"Carlos is behind that bush," she told Albert. "I saw him run over there."

"Let's get him!" Albert cheered.

Marika and Albert ran to the bush.

Carlos heard them coming. He didn't want to be tagged. So he ran off to find a new hiding place.

SPLAT! Carlos tripped on his shoelace.

"We found you!" Marika and Albert cheered. They tagged Carlos on the arm.

"You only got me because I fell," Carlos told Marika and Albert.

"You should wear shoes like mine," Marika told him. "They don't have laces."

"No way!" Carlos shouted. "Those are ballet slippers. And they're pink!"

"Okay," Marika said. "But then you'll always trip. And you'll always lose at hide-and-seek."

"Albert found *you*, too," Carlos reminded her.

Marika didn't say anything else.

Ring! Ring! The bell rang. School was starting.

The first graders ran inside as fast as they could. They couldn't wait to find out what fun Miss Popper had planned for them inside Appleville Elementary School!

Chapter 2
What Am I?

"I hate hide-and-seek!" Carlos told his friends Justine and J.B. "Someone always finds me."

"You should have climbed the tree, like me," Justine said.

"And me," J.B. added.

"Nobody found us!" J.B. and Justine said together.

"We would have found you, but the bell rang," Albert told Justine and J.B. "We didn't have enough time."

"You wouldn't have *tagged* me," J.B. answered. "I was way up high. Even if you saw me, you wouldn't have been able to climb up there."

Albert knew that was true. J.B. was the best climber in the class.

"I would never climb a tree," Carlos said. "I don't like being up high."

7

"Not even in a plane?" J.B. asked.

Carlos shook his head. "Nope."

"I love airplanes," Marika told Carlos. "I like to look down at the clouds."

"I like to look *up* at the clouds," Carlos said. "Yesterday I saw one that was shaped like a cow. It was *moo*-ving across the sky."

The other kids laughed.

Miss Popper smiled at her class. "Speaking of clouds, it's Marika's turn to do the weather chart," she said.

Marika stood up. She twirled over to the weather chart. Then she placed a gray, felt cloud on the chart.

"Today the weather is cloudy and cool," she told the class.

"Why do you dance everywhere?" J.B. asked Marika.

"Because I'm a ballerina," she answered.

"No, you're not," Carlos said. "You just take ballet *classes*."

"It's the same thing," Marika told Carlos. She stuck out her tongue.

"Marika!" Miss Popper said. "We don't do that in first grade."

Marika frowned. "I'm sorry," she said.

"*You're* sorry. But can you guess what *I* am?" Carlos asked the class.

He got on the floor, and rolled around and around.

"Ruff! Ruff!" Carlos barked like a dog.

"What are you?" Justine asked him.

"I'm a hot dog on a roll!" Carlos joked.

The kids laughed. Then they waited for Miss Popper to tell Carlos that first graders don't roll around on the floor.

Instead, Miss Popper told Carlos to stay right where he was.

"Don't get up," Miss Popper said. "You're in the right place."

"For what?" Carlos asked.

"You'll see!" Miss Popper said.

Chapter 3
Stop, Drop, and Roll

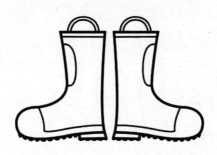

"Today, we're going to learn about fire safety," Miss Popper told the class. "Do you know what to do if there is a fire?"

"My family has fire drills," Albert said. "We practice leaving the house, fast. If a real fire happens, we know what to do!"

"Very good!" Miss Popper told Albert. "But what if your *clothes* catch on fire?"

The kids all stopped smiling. They looked very scared.

That's because they *were* scared. Even J.B. And he was hardly ever scared.

"Don't worry," Miss Popper told them. "I'm going to teach you how to stay safe."

That made J.B. feel better. *But only a little bit.*

"Justine and J.B.," Miss Popper said. "Will you please go to the front of the room?"

Justine and J.B. stood up.

"Now, pretend your pants have caught on fire," Miss Popper told them.

J.B. and Justine began to jump up and down.

"Ahh! Ouch!" J.B. shouted. He shook his legs.

"Hot! Hot!" Justine screamed. "My pants are on fire!"

"Great!" Miss Popper cheered. "Now J.B., stop where you are."

J.B. stopped moving.

Then Miss Popper said, "Justine, drop to the floor."

Justine dropped to her knees.

"Carlos, roll," Miss Popper said.

Carlos rolled over and over.

"That's what you do if your clothes catch fire," Miss Popper said. "Stop, drop, and roll. That will put the fire out."

"That's all you have to do?" Albert asked.

"That's it," Miss Popper answered. "Why don't you give it a try?"

The kids all began practicing. They stopped where they stood. They dropped to the floor. Then they rolled.

"Stop. Drop. Roll!" they cheered. "Stop. Drop. Roll!"

"Great job, everyone!" Miss Popper said. "Now, go back to your seats."

The first graders sat down at their desks. They were still excited from stopping, dropping, and rolling.

Then Miss Popper told them something even *more* exciting.

"Tomorrow we will be going on a field trip!" she said.

"Where are we going?" J.B. asked.

Miss Popper smiled. "It's a surprise. But I promise you'll love it!"

Chapter 4
Firefighters Don't Wear Tutus!

After school, the first graders all went to J.B.'s backyard.

"Where do you think we're going on our field trip tomorrow?" Justine asked.

"Maybe we're going to the library," Albert suggested.

"Or the zoo," Carlos said.

"Or the art museum," J.B. added.

"We won't know until tomorrow," Marika said. "So let's stop talking, and start playing!"

"Okay. But what should we play?" Justine asked.

"Let's pretend we're firefighters!" Albert suggested.

"Great idea!" Justine cheered. "Marika, go to the top of the slide. I'll climb up and pretend to save you from a fire."

Marika shook her head. "I want to be the firefighter," she told Justine.

"You can't be a firefighter," Carlos told Marika.

"Why not?" Marika demanded.

"Because firefighters don't wear tutus!" Carlos said.

"I can be a firefighter if I want to be!" Marika shouted at Carlos.

"No, you can't!" Carlos shouted back.

"Yes, she can!" J.B.'s little brother, Mikey, yelled.

J.B. got very angry. He hated when his little brother butted in.

"Go away, Mikey," J.B. told him. "I don't want you to play with my friends. This is a big kid game."

"Marika is *my* friend too," Mikey told his big brother. "She'll save me!"

"I sure will," Marika agreed. "Climb to the top of the slide, Mikey. Then, I — *Firefighter Marika* — will rescue you."

Mikey raced over to the wooden slide. He climbed all the way to the top.

"Help! Help!" Mikey shouted. He pretended to be scared.

Firefighter Marika danced over to the slide. She climbed up and rescued Mikey from the pretend fire.

"Wheee!" Mikey and Marika squealed as they slid down the slide together.

J.B. ran to the monkey bars. He climbed up. And up. And up.

"Firefighter Carlos, come save me!" J.B. called down to his friend.

Carlos looked up and shook his head.

"Firefighter Justine can rescue you," Carlos shouted up to J.B. "I'll stay down here. I can put out the flames with the fire hose."

"I'm on my way!" Justine shouted. She raced up the monkey bars. Justine was a great climber. She was almost as good as J.B.!

"Ruff! Ruff!"

Just then, J.B.'s dog, Frisky, ran out into the yard. He wanted to play, too!

Bam! Frisky ran right into Carlos. He knocked him down. Carlos was covered in ooey-gooey mud. Yuck!

The kids all stopped playing. They stared at Carlos.

At first Carlos didn't say anything.

Uh-oh! Was Carlos mad at Frisky?

No. Carlos wasn't mad at all. In fact, he was laughing.

"I love dogs," he said happily. "I love *all* animals."

"I hope you love baths too," Marika joked. "Because you really need one!"

Carlos giggled. Then he stroked Frisky's head.

"You can be our pretend firehouse dog," Carlos told him.

Slurp. Frisky licked Carlos right on the nose!

Carlos giggled. "I knew you would like that," he said.

Chapter 5
Field Trip!

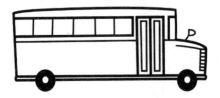

"Good morning, everybody!" Miss Popper greeted the kids as they walked into Room 102. "Do you remember what today is?"

"Field trip day!" the kids cheered.

"Does everyone have a note from a parent?" Miss Popper asked them.

"I do!" Carlos shouted out.

"Me too!" Justine said.

One by one the kids handed Miss Popper their signed notes.

"Now we can go on our trip!" Miss Popper told them.

"Will you tell us where we're going?" J.B. asked Miss Popper.

"You'll see when we get there," she told him. "Let's get on the bus!"

The first graders all ran outside. They got on the bus.

Justine started bouncing in her seat. She was not good at keeping still when she was excited.

"Let's go! Let's go! Let's go!" Justine chanted as she bounced up and down.

"We'll leave as soon as you buckle your seat belt," Miss Popper told her.

Snap. Justine buckled up right away!

"Okay, Mr. Wheeler," Miss Popper told the bus driver. "We're ready!"

Mr. Wheeler drove through the town. The bus passed Mr. Furman's pet store.

"That's where one of our class gerbils, Happy, came from!" Carlos shouted as they passed the store.

The bus went around the traffic circle near the diner.

"I love the hamburgers there," Marika told Justine.

"The French fries are yummy, too," Justine said.

Then the bus turned left at the supermarket, and right at the candy store.

Finally, the yellow school bus stopped in front of a big, brick building. There were two fire trucks parked inside a big red garage.

"Our field trip is to the firehouse!"
Albert figured out.

"This is going to be so cool!" Justine
cheered.

Chapter 6
Clang, Clang, Wheee, Ruff!

A real, live firefighter came out to greet the first graders. He wore black rubber boots and a yellow helmet.

"I'm Firefighter Tom," he said. "Welcome to our firehouse!"

"I'm glad I wore my yellow tutu," Marika told Firefighter Tom. "It matches your helmet."

Firefighter Tom laughed. "It sure does," he told her.

"Can we take a ride in the fire truck?" Justine asked him.

Firefighter Tom shook his head. "We only take the truck out when there is trouble. But there are a lot of other fun things you can do while you are here."

Firefighter Tom showed the first graders around the firehouse. He let them pretend to be firefighters.

Marika and Albert rang the fire bell. *Clang! Clang!*

Justine and J.B slid down the fire pole. *Wheee!*

But Carlos wasn't happy.

"What's wrong?" Firefighter Tom asked.

"I wanted to see animals on our field trip," Carlos said.

"I can help you with that," Firefighter Tom told Carlos. He whistled loudly. "Sparky, come here!"

A big spotted dog raced over to Firefighter Tom.

"A real fire dog!" Carlos shouted. Now he was happy, too!

"Ruff!" Sparky barked.

"Sparky loves kids," Firefighter Tom told the class.

"You're lucky to have such a nice pet," Carlos said.

"Do any of *you* have pets?" Firefighter Tom asked the kids.

J.B. raised his hand. "I have a dog."

Firefighter Tom handed J.B. an orange-and-silver sticker.

"Put this on your front door," Firefighter Tom told J.B.

"Why?" J.B. asked.

"The sticker tells firefighters to look for your dog if there is a fire," Firefighter Tom said. "Dogs and cats sometimes hide when they're afraid."

"So you have to play hide-and-seek with them," Justine said.

Firefighter Tom laughed. "Something like that," he said.

"You wouldn't have any trouble finding Carlos during a fire," Marika told Firefighter Tom. "He's a terrible hider."

"Marika, that's not nice." Miss Popper scolded. "Please tell Carlos you're sorry."

"I'm sorry, Carlos," Marika said. But she didn't sound like she meant it.

Marika had made Carlos feel really bad. He hated the way she always made fun of him.

"I'll show her," Carlos whispered to Sparky. "I'll find the best hiding spot ever!"

"Ruff!" Sparky barked. Then she licked Carlos on the nose.

"Come on," Firefighter Tom said to the

kids and to Miss Popper. "Let me show you our kitchen. We can have a snack."

"I hope there are cookies," Albert said.

The kids and Miss Popper all followed Firefighter Tom. Well, *almost* all of them, anyway. Carlos ran off to hide!

Chapter 7
Where's Carlos?

Ring! Ring! Suddenly, the alarm sounded.

"I'm sorry, boys and girls," Firefighter Tom said. "That bell means someone needs our help. We have to go."

The kids watched as the firefighters put on their suits and helmets, and climbed into the big red fire engine. The siren whirred as the truck sped away.

"That was an exciting field trip!" Miss Popper said. "But now we have to get on the bus. It's time to go back to school."

Justine, J.B., Marika, and Albert headed out to the yellow bus.

"Come on, Carlos," Miss Popper called into the firehouse. "You have to say good-bye to Sparky and go back to school."

But Carlos didn't answer.

"Where's Carlos?" Miss Popper asked the other first graders.

"He was just here," Albert said. Then he thought for a minute. "Wasn't he?" he asked his friends.

"I'm not sure," J.B. said.

"I don't remember seeing him in the kitchen," Justine said.

"Or when the firefighters were getting on their truck," Marika added.

Miss Popper frowned. "Oh, dear," she said. "We need to find him before we can go back to school."

"That won't be hard," Marika said. "I can always find Carlos."

The kids searched the firehouse.

They looked in the kitchen. No Carlos.

They looked in the computer room. No Carlos.

They looked in the room where the firefighters slept. No Carlos.

They even looked in Sparky's doghouse. But the kids couldn't find Carlos anywhere.

"This is the best Carlos has ever hidden," Justine said.

"He is definitely winning this game of hide-and-seek," Marika agreed.

The first graders thought that was really great.

But Miss Popper did not look happy about it at all.

Chapter 8
Tree Trouble

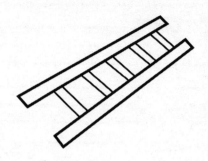

Carlos was *very* happy.

He had found a really great hiding place. No one had found him. Not his teacher. Not his friends. Not even the firefighters.

Carlos was hiding in the fire truck!

The fire truck stopped in front of a house. Carlos peeked out the window. He tried to see the flames.

But there was no fire. There was only a

little girl standing near a tree with her mother. The girl was crying.

"My kitty climbed up that tree," the little girl told the firefighters. "And now she can't get down."

"Don't worry," Firefighter Tom told her. "We'll save her."

"Oh, thank you," the girl's mother answered. "The kitten's name is Daisy. She really needs your help!"

Carlos peeked out the window of the truck. He watched as Firefighter Tom placed a ladder beside the tree. Then he began to climb. Up, up, up he went. He stopped when he was as high up as the kitten.

"Here, kitty, kitty," Firefighter Tom called to Daisy.

Daisy took one look at Firefighter Tom and ran higher up the tree.

"She won't come to me," Firefighter Tom called down to the woman. "I think I scared her."

Carlos could understand that. Firefighter Tom was very tall. And he

was wearing a scary black-and-yellow firefighter uniform. Daisy probably thought he was a giant monster.

A giant monster would scare anyone.

Of course, Firefighter Tom wasn't really a monster. He was a firefighter. But Daisy didn't know that.

The little girl began to sob. "If you can't help Daisy, who can?" she asked.

Chapter 9
Carlos to the Rescue

There *was* one person who could help Daisy. That person was Carlos.

He was just a first grader. He wasn't big and tall. He wasn't wearing heavy, black boots, or a big, scary helmet.

But Carlos knew Daisy wouldn't be afraid of him.

Carlos looked up. He could see Daisy sitting on a branch. She seemed very far away. But he could still hear her.

"Meow, meow, meow." It sounded like Daisy was crying.

Carlos knew exactly how she felt. He didn't like being up high, either.

But Daisy *was* up high. And she needed his help.

Carlos began to climb out of the truck.

All of the firefighters were looking up at Daisy. They did not notice Carlos running to the tree.

"Meow, meow," Daisy cried again.

Carlos raced around to the back of the tree.

The firefighters could not see him there. But Daisy could.

"Meow, meow," she cried to Carlos.

"I'll save you, Daisy," Carlos called up to the kitten.

Carlos began to climb the tree. Even though he was scared, he put his foot on one branch.

Then another.

And another.

"Just don't look down," Carlos told himself.

Finally, Carlos reached the branch where Daisy was sitting.

"Here, kitty, kitty," he called to her.

Daisy looked at Carlos. "Meow," she purred. Then she tiptoed across the branch and into his arms.

"I've got her!" Carlos shouted to the people below.

Firefighter Tom looked up in the tree. He was very surprised.

"Carlos!" he shouted. "What are you doing here?"

"Saving Daisy," Carlos answered.

"But why aren't you with your class?" Firefighter Tom asked.

"I was hiding in the truck," Carlos told him. "You drove away before I could get out."

"I see," Firefighter Tom said. "Why don't you bring Daisy down now? We can talk about this later."

That's when Carlos made a big mistake. He looked down.

The ground seemed very far away.

Now Daisy wasn't the only one in the tree who was scared.

"I can't climb down," Carlos said. "I'm afraid. I might fall."

"Stay right there!" Firefighter Tom called to Carlos. "I'll come get you both."

Firefighter Tom climbed higher on the ladder. Then he reached out and took hold of Carlos.

Carlos held Daisy tightly. Firefighter Tom carried them both down the ladder.

Carlos was happy to be back on the ground again!

The little girl was very happy to have Daisy back.

"You saved my kitten!" she told Carlos.

"You're a hero," the girl's mother said.

Firefighter Tom shook Carlos's hand. Then he put his big yellow helmet on Carlos's head.

"Now you're a junior firefighter!" he told Carlos.

Carlos smiled. A junior firefighter. That was so cool. The other kids were going to be really proud of him. He just knew it.

Chapter 10
The Hero Comes Back

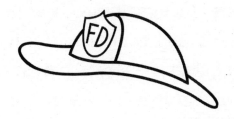

Carlos was right. The first graders were excited to hear about Carlos and Daisy.

"You climbed up a tree?" Justine asked him.

"Yep." Carlos nodded.

"Wow!" J.B. said. "You never did that before."

"I know," Carlos said. "Daisy was so small. I had to help her."

"Kittens are cute," Marika said.

"Were you scared up there?" Albert asked Carlos.

"A little," Carlos admitted. "But it wasn't as bad as I thought it would be."

"Maybe you'll climb a tree the next time we play hide-and-seek," Albert said.

Carlos shrugged. "Maybe. Or maybe not. I'm not telling."

"Why not?" Marika asked.

"Because if I tell, you'll know where to find me," Carlos said.

"Very smart," Albert told him.

"Carlos won't be playing hide-and-seek during recess for a while," Miss Popper said to the class.

"I won't?" Carlos asked his teacher. "Why not?"

"Even junior firefighters have to follow the rules," Miss Popper told Carlos.

"You should not have hidden in that fire truck. You should have stayed with the class."

Carlos frowned. But he didn't say anything. What could he say? Miss Popper was right.

"You won't be allowed to go on the playground for one week," Miss Popper told him. "You will have to stay in the classroom with me."

That was not good news. Carlos liked playing on the playground after lunch.

Still, Carlos was happy. He was glad he'd gotten to ride in the fire truck.

He was glad he'd climbed a tree.

But mostly, he was glad he'd saved Daisy.

"Okay, everyone," Miss Popper said to the kids. "Now that we're all here, let's

get on the bus. It's time to go back to school."

"I wonder what we'll do when we get back," Marika said to Albert.

"I bet Miss Popper has some more surprises for us," Albert told her.

"What kind of surprises?" Justine wondered.

"I don't know," Albert said. "But I'm sure they will be good. First grade is full of surprises!"

Here's a sneak peek at the next book:
The 100th Day

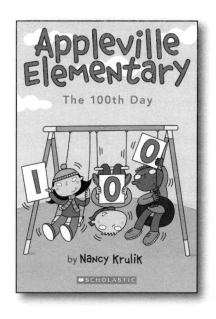

"Are you going to tell us about the one hundred days celebration now?" Justine asked Miss Popper.

"One hundred is a big number," Marika said. "It should be a *big* celebration."

"It will be," Miss Popper told her. "It will fill the whole gym."

"What's big enough to fill the gym?" Albert asked.

"A museum," Miss Popper said.

The kids all looked at her.

"A museum is coming to our school?" Carlos asked.

"With dinosaur bones?" J.B. asked.

"Or paintings?" Marika wondered.

"If that's what you want," Miss Popper told them.

"I don't understand," Albert said.

"Our school is making a One Hundred Days of School Museum," Miss Popper explained. "Each class will have its own table. And each table will have one hundred things on it."

"What hundred things will *we* have on our table?" Carlos asked.

"That's up to all of you," Miss Popper said.

"Our display has to be the best," Marika said.

"It will be," J.B. promised her.